CATHERINE AND LAURENCE ANHOLT have collaborated
on 80 best-selling children's titles, which have been
published in 23 countries around the world.
Their books have won numerous awards including the prestigious
Nestlé Smarties Gold Award on two occasions.
Laurence was recently included in the *Independent* on *Sunday's*
Top Ten Children's Authors.

Many of their ideas spring directly from family life.
The inspiration for the stories of the mischievous twins Chimp and Zee
came from the misadventures of their own twins, Tom and Maddy.

The Anholts live in a rambling farmhouse near Lyme Regis in Dorset.

For peace in stormy times.

Meet Chimp and Zee at the Anholt website – www.anholt.co.uk

Chimp and Zee and the Big Storm copyright © Frances Lincoln Limited 2002
Text copyright © Laurence Anholt 2002
Illustrations copyright © Catherine Anholt 2002

The right of Laurence Anholt to be identified as the Author
and of Catherine Anholt to be identified as the Illustrator
of this work has been asserted by them in accordance
with the Copyright, Designs and Patents Act 1988.

First published in Great Britain in 2002 by Frances Lincoln Children's Books,
4 Torriano Mews, Torriano Avenue, London NW5 2RZ
www.franceslincoln.com

First paperback edition 2004

British Library Cataloguing in Publication Data available on request

ISBN 1-84507-069-0

Set in Chimp and Zee
Designed by Sarah Massini

Printed in China
3 5 7 9 8 6 4

Chimp and Zee
and the BIG STORM

Catherine and
Laurence Anholt

FRANCES LINCOLN CHILDREN'S BOOKS

This is Chimp,   this is Zee,

on a *stormy* day in the coconut tree.

The rain rattles on the roof.
The wind whistles round the windows.
It is too stormy to go out and play.
Chimp and Zee do not want
to do anything together.

They squibble and
squabble and drive
everyone bananas.
Until...
SNAP!

"Chimp did it."

"Zee did it."

"I wasn't even there."

"Zee did it."

"Chimp did it."

"It's just NOT FAIR!"

"Oh you chumpy chimps," sighs Mumkey.

Papakey looks at the windy garden.
"Goodness!" he says. "We've left the washing outside.
I will fetch it, before it blows away."

Chimp and Zee want to go out too.
They are not afraid of the Big Storm.
"You must hold tight to Papakey," says Mumkey,
"and you must not squibble and squabble."

It is VERY windy outside.
Chimp and Zee do NOT hold tight to Papakey.

They DO squibble
and squabble.

They monkey about
and drive
Papakey bananas.

Then, WHOOSH!

A pair of Mumkey's pants blows right up into a tree.

"Chimp did it."
"Zee did it."
"I wasn't even there."
"Zee did it."
"Chimp did it."
"It's just NOT FAIR!"

"Oh you chumpy chimps," sighs Papakey.

Then Chimp and Zee try to help. They fold a big sheet.

But suddenly, there is another gust of wind...

Whoo-OOSH!!

When Papakey turns around, the sheet is flying in the air like a kite...

and so are Chimp and Zee!

Mumkey hears shouting.
She sees Chimp and Zee
float past the window.

"Come down!"
cry Mumkey and Papakey.
"Little monkeys
should not fly."

"Wa! Wa! WAA!" shouts Chimp.
"Woo! Hoo! HOO!" shouts Zee.

The Big Storm carries
Chimp and Zee out of the garden.
Past the dancing trees...

higher...

and HIGHER...

AND **HIGHER!**

Way above Jungletown.

"My goodness!
Those little monkeys are
heading straight for the sea!"
shouts a shopkeeper.

"Help, help, help!" shouts Chimp.
"Put us down!" squeals Zee.

But the Big Storm
will not put them down.
It sweeps them through
the dark sky...
...closer and closer to
the Very Dangerous Cliffs.

"Chimp and Zee will
be lost at sea," says the
old lighthouse keeper sadly.

Here are Mumkey and Papakey, chasing the flyaway twins.

Faster, faster, faster!

Papakey pedals up the hill. Right to the top
of the Very Dangerous Cliffs. But he is too late!
Chimp and Zee have already gone...
high above the wild and wicked waves.

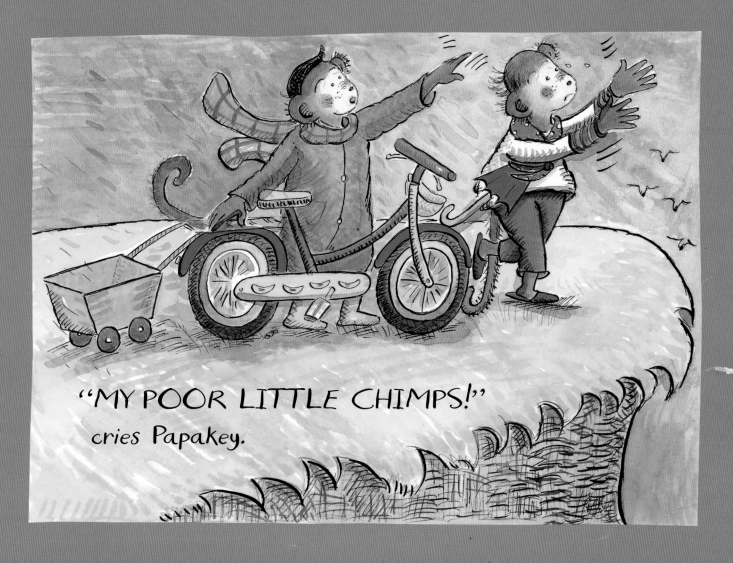

"MY POOR LITTLE CHIMPS!"
cries Papakey.

O-OO-M!!,,

booms the Big Storm.

Quick as lightning, Mumkey does an amazing thing
— she grabs her umbrella and
climbs high onto Papakey's shoulders.

Mumkey stretches...

higher and higher

and HIGHER.

She pulls down her sheet and ...

her wet and windy Chimp and Zee.

"Chimp did it."

"Zee did it."

"I wasn't even there."

"Zee did it."

"Chimp did it."

"It's just NOT FAIR!"

"Oh you chumpy chimps!" laughs Mumkey.

Then Papakey hurries through the flooded fields.

Past the rushing river. Back to their home in the coconut tree.

Quick! Up the ladder!
Slam the door!

"We do not want
the Big Storm in here."

Then Mumkey lights the stove.

Papakey fries hot bananas.

Chimp and Zee cuddle together,

snug as twins in a rug;

and they sing songs together,

all through the wild afternoon...

rock-a-bye monkey, on the tree top...

"Families can be stormy sometimes," smiles Papakey.
"Yes," says Mumkey, "but whatever
the weather, we'll always be together."

Mumkey and Papakey and...

Chimp and Zee

as the sun comes out
in the coconut tree.

MORE CHIMP AND ZEE BOOKS
FROM FRANCES LINCOLN

CHIMP AND ZEE
Catherine and Laurence Anholt

Welcome to the wonderful world of Chimp and Zee,
the cheekiest, most loveable twins in the whole of Jungletown.
Winner of the 2001 Nestle Smarties Book Award, this is
a children's classic in the making. Also available as a board book.

CHIMP AND ZEE'S NOISY BOOK
Catherine and Laurence Anholt

Bark, clap, toot and roar along with Chimp and Zee
in this noisy board book starring the most loveable twins in Jungletown.

MONKEY ABOUT WITH CHIMP AND ZEE
Catherine and Laurence Anholt

Touch the book, lick the book, even KISS the book!
Monkey around with Chimp and Zee in the ultimate interactive board book.

Frances Lincoln titles are available from all good bookshops.
You can also buy books and find out more about your favourite titles,
authors and illustrators on our website: www.franceslincoln.com